Mother turns toward him. "The rules exist because we don't get second chances."

He says, "I just don't like pretending the world is smaller than it is."

Mother presses close, surrounding him with herself. "I don't like pretending it isn't dangerous."

The Taking

The Taking

by

Steven K. Dunn

THE TAKING: Steven K. Dunn

1st Ed.

ISBN: 978-1-957173-50-4

For Bob—

May she hunt well …

Contents

Chapter 1
The Shape of a Life

I wake because my brother is already awake. I can tell without opening my eyes. He has a way of shifting that sends a familiar ripple through those nearest him, like a reminder passed hand to hand. When I don't

respond right away, he nudges me—not impatiently, just enough to say come back.

"You're doing it again," he says.

"I was resting," I answer.

"You were drifting."

"That's the same thing."

He presses closer, amused. "Only if you don't wander off."

I open my eyes—though eyes isn't quite right; it's more a sharpening of awareness, a pulling of the world into focus. Light has

arrived. Not gradually, not politely. One moment the world was folded inward and dim, the next it is simply on, bright and clear and full of detail.

Morning.

Around us, the Many is already stirring. Movement overlaps movement. Familiar presences brush past me—kin, neighbors, those I've known all my life without ever needing to mark where one ends and another begins. We live close. We always have. Space exists, but closeness is how we stay oriented.

My sister slips in on my other side, quick and deliberate. "You're both in my way," she says, which means she's pleased we're here.

"You could go around," my brother replies.

"I could," she agrees. "But I won't."

Mother moves through us not long after, steady and unhurried. She doesn't announce herself. She never needs to. The way she moves changes the texture of the world nearby— calmer, more ordered.

The Taking

She brushes against each of us in turn, a habit so old none of us remember when it started.

"All of you are up early," she says.

"You say that every day," my sister replies.

"And one day," Mother says, "you'll be right."

My brother laughs. I feel it in the way his movement loosens, careless for a moment. Above us, the world feels lighter. Not safer—

just easier. Below, it thickens, tangles, grows quieter.

We drift upward with the rest of the Many, not because anyone tells us to, but because the day seems to ask it of us.

Something begins to arrive from Above. It always does, though never exactly the same way twice. Tiny fragments descend, patient and numerous. They carry warmth with them, reassurance. The Many spreads instinctively, gathering without crowding, taking without hoarding.

The Taking

"This one's mine," my sister declares, darting toward a fragment.

"You don't own anything that falls from Above," my brother tells her.

"I touched it first."

"That's not how it works."

Mother watches the exchange with a look that is half fondness, half vigilance. "Enough," she says. "There's no shortage."

She's right. There rarely is.

I take my time, letting the fragments drift closer rather than chasing them. My brother has always said I move like I'm listening for something no one else hears. I don't know if that's true. I only know that rushing has never felt natural to me.

Nearby, an elder glides past—Old Tareth, whose movements have grown slower over time, not from weakness but from deliberation. He watches the Many the way Mother does, with attention that borders on counting.

The Taking

"Bright hours today," he remarks, more to the world than to anyone in particular.

"Are they ever not?" my sister asks.

He pauses. "Some are brighter than others."

Mother's attention sharpens at that. "You feel something?"

Tareth considers. "I feel what I always feel. Which is to say—nothing I trust."

No one presses him. We all understand the limits of that kind of knowing. The day continues. Conversations overlap and drift

apart. Someone nearby is recounting a story we've all heard before, about the time they nearly lost their bearings and ended up far from everyone they knew. It's told lightly, with humor, but I notice how Mother positions herself closer as it's told.

"Don't go so far," she says quietly, to no one and everyone.

"I won't," my brother replies automatically.

My sister doesn't answer, which means she's thinking about it.

The Taking

The Taking is never named directly. It doesn't need to be. It lives in the spaces between instructions, in the way we cluster without discussing why, in the subtle rules everyone follows and no one claims to have made. Stay within sight. Don't linger alone. Don't be last to leave.

Don't be first to arrive.

Every so often, someone is gone. Not dramatically. Not loudly. Simply… not present where they once were. When it happens, there's a brief stillness. A recalibration.

Someone might say, "They must have drifted too far," or, "I thought they were with you." No one asks how. No one asks where.

Life resumes.

Today, no one is missing. At least, not today. Mother remains watchful anyway. She always is. She positions herself so she can see all of us at once, a habit she pretends is casual.

"You're counting," my sister says softly, pressing close.

"I always count," Mother replies.

The Taking

"You didn't used to."

Mother doesn't answer that.

The world holds steady through the bright hours. Light remains constant. The fragments from Above slow, then stop. The Many settles into a gentler rhythm—less gathering, more drifting. Conversations soften. Movement becomes less purposeful.

I stay near my family, not because I've been told to, but because it feels right.

"Do you ever wonder," my brother says suddenly, "if the world has an end?"

My sister snorts. "Of course it does."

"Have you seen it?"

"No."

"Then how do you know?"

She bumps him lightly. "Because everything ends."

Mother listens without interrupting.

The Taking

"I think," my brother continues, "that if you kept going long enough, you'd find something new. Something different."

"Or you'd find nothing," my sister replies. "And then you'd be alone."

"That's not the same thing."

"It is if you don't come back."

Mother finally speaks. "Curiosity is not the problem," she says. "Distance is."

The conversation drifts away from that point, but the weight of it remains. As the light

begins to change—subtly, almost imperceptibly—I feel a tightening I can't name. Not fear. Something quieter. The sense that the world is adjusting itself around us.

Mother shifts position.

"So soon?" my sister asks.

"Just in case," Mother answers.

Nothing happens. Which, in its own way, is reassuring. The Many gathers again as the brightness begins to withdraw. Evening doesn't arrive so much as assert itself. The world dims

all at once, folding back into itself. We cluster close. The habit is old enough to feel instinctive.

"Tomorrow," my brother says, "I'm going to go a little farther."

Mother's presence sharpens immediately. "You're not."

"I'll stay where you can see me."

"That's not the rule."

"It's just a rule."

Mother turns toward him fully now. "The rules exist because we don't get second chances."

He softens at that, the recklessness draining out of him. "I know," he says. "I just don't like pretending the world is smaller than it is."

Mother presses close, surrounding him with herself. "I don't like pretending it isn't dangerous."

Silence settles over us—not awkward, not heavy. Just shared. The world holds. No one is taken.

Not today.

And because of that, it is easy—dangerously easy—to believe tomorrow will be the same.

"You're hovering," my sister tells her one day.

Mother doesn't deny it.

"You didn't used to."

"I did," Mother says. "You just didn't notice."

Chapter 2

What We Learn to Avoid

The days that follow are not remarkable. That is the strangest part. Nothing announces itself as different. Light still arrives when it always has. The world still carries us when we allow it to. The fragments still come from

Above—sometimes plentiful, sometimes sparse, but never absent long enough to cause alarm.

If anything, life becomes more careful. Which is not the same thing as fearful.

My brother keeps his promise and does not go farther, though I can feel the restraint in him the way you feel a held breath. He moves in wider arcs than before, testing distance without crossing it, glancing back often enough that Mother notices but does not comment.

The Taking

My sister notices everything. She notices how often Mother adjusts her position. How she always places herself between us and the open stretches. How she waits until all of us are close before allowing herself to rest.

"You're hovering," my sister tells her one day.

Mother doesn't deny it. "I prefer awareness."

"You didn't used to."

"I did," Mother says. "You just didn't notice."

That answer satisfies no one, but we let it stand. The Many adapts the way it always has—without discussion. Clusters grow tighter. Empty stretches linger longer before anyone drifts into them. Elders reposition themselves in places where they can see more, hear more, sense more. It is all very subtle. If you weren't living inside it, you might think nothing had changed at all.

The Taking

I spend more time listening. Not to sounds—
there are none in the way the word suggests—
but to shifts in attention, in pressure, in the
way movement sometimes falters before
correcting itself. There are moments when the
world feels thinner, stretched taut, as if
something has passed through recently and left
a faint echo behind.

I don't mention it. I'm not sure how.

One afternoon, as the brightness holds
steady longer than usual, I drift with Old

Tareth along the lower reaches where growth thickens and the world slows.

"You're watching again," he observes.

"So are you," I reply.

He gives what might be a smile. "That's my job."

"What are you watching for?"

He considers. "Patterns."

"Do you see any?"

"Yes."

The Taking

"And?"

"And I don't like them."

I wait. He does not elaborate. Nearby, a group of younger ones weave through each other, reckless with joy, bumping and spinning, chasing nothing at all. One of them strays farther than the rest, laughing—carefree, unafraid. A nearby elder shifts immediately, blocking the open stretch without saying a word. The younger one veers back, confusion flickering briefly before it dissolves

into something else—acceptance, maybe. Or habit.

Life resumes.

Later, as the world begins its slow dimming, my brother drifts closer to me. "Do you ever feel like we're pretending?" he asks.

"Pretending what?"

"That this is normal."

I think about it. "It is normal."

He frowns. "That doesn't mean it's right."

The Taking

My sister overhears and joins us. "Normal just means you survived it," she says. "So far."

Mother arrives just in time to hear that. "That's enough," she says, though her tone is gentle. "Speculation doesn't keep anyone safe."

My brother's frustration sharpens. "Neither does pretending we don't see what's happening."

Mother holds his gaze. "We see it," she says quietly. "We just don't let it consume us."

"Why not?"

"Because that's how you stop living long before you're taken."

The words settle heavily between us. Taken. No one flinches. The word is part of our language, the way storms are part of other worlds' languages. Something that happens. Something you prepare for without believing it will be today.

Night—if it can be called that—comes abruptly. The world dims all at once, as it always does, folding inward like a held thought. The Many draws close again,

clustering by instinct rather than instruction. I find myself pressed between my sister and my brother, the three of us forming a familiar line. Mother positions herself just beyond us, her awareness extending outward.

"Tell me something," my sister says suddenly.

"What?" my brother asks.

"Something from before you started worrying all the time."

He snorts. "That narrows it down."

"Just do it."

He thinks for a moment. "Do you remember when you got stuck?"

I stiffen. "I wasn't stuck."

"You wedged yourself somewhere you couldn't move," he corrects. "That's stuck."

"I was exploring."

"You panicked," my sister adds.

"I did not."

The Taking

Mother's attention flickers toward us, but she allows the memory.

"You cried," my brother says, warming to the story now. "You called for Mother like the world was ending."

"It was ending," I protest. "For me."

"And then," my sister continues, "Mother reached you in about half a breath and pulled you free."

Mother inclines her head slightly. "I told you not to go there."

"You tell us not to go anywhere," my brother says.

"Yes," Mother replies. "And yet."

We share a quiet moment of laughter, the tension easing just enough to breathe again. For a while, the world feels almost kind. That is when the first warning comes. Not a disappearance. Not yet. Just a change. A sudden tightening of the medium around us. A subtle but unmistakable displacement somewhere nearby. The kind that makes elders still and younger ones instinctively drift closer.

The Taking

Mother shifts immediately. "Closer," she says. We obey without question. Nothing happens. The pressure fades. The world relaxes. Someone laughs, embarrassed.

"False alarm," my sister says.

Mother doesn't correct her. But she doesn't move away either.

Later, when the brightness returns and the day begins again, I notice something missing. Not someone. A space. A familiar cluster that doesn't form. A place where voices used to overlap, now quieter than it should be.

"Where's—" I begin.

My sister stops me with a look. "Don't," she says softly. "They might just be elsewhere."

Might. The word hangs there. Mother says nothing. She simply adjusts her position again, widening her watch. Life continues. It always does. But the spaces between us are harder to ignore now. The rules feel tighter, more urgent. Conversations stop more abruptly when elders pass. Joy is still there—but it is careful, contained, as if everyone understands that too much of it invites attention.

The Taking

That night, as the world dims once more, my brother leans close. "If it happens," he says quietly, "stay with Mother."

I don't like the way he says if. "Don't talk like that," I tell him.

He presses his side to mine. "I'm not planning on going anywhere."

Neither was anyone else.

The world folds inward around us. The Many clusters. The light fades. Nothing happens. And yet. For the first time, I fall into

rest wondering not whether the Taking will come again—but who it will choose.

Old Tareth drifts nearer, his movements heavy with something like sorrow.

"It was fast," he says quietly. "Too fast to feel."

My sister rounds on him. "You didn't see it."

"No," he agrees. "But I felt the absence."

Chapter 3

The Space Where Someone Was

The day begins gently. That is what makes it unbearable. Light arrives and the world settles into its familiar clarity, and for a moment— just a moment—I believe we were wrong. That

the tightening, the vigilance, the half-finished conversations were all caution grown too large in our minds.

My brother is already awake, drifting nearby, tracing small, absent patterns through the medium like he's thinking with his body.

"You didn't rest," I tell him.

"I did," he says. "Just not deeply."

My sister presses in on my other side. "You never rest deeply," she says. "You hover."

"I observe."

"You worry."

He doesn't deny it.

Mother is close but not hovering—she's learned how to look relaxed without actually relaxing. Her awareness stretches outward in careful arcs, touching the edges of our small cluster, then returning. Old Tareth passes nearby and inclines himself slightly toward Mother.

"Quiet day," he says.

"So far," Mother replies.

We drift upward with the Many as the brightness holds. The fragments from Above arrive later than usual, but when they do, they are plentiful. Warmth spreads. Movement loosens. Laughter—real laughter—ripples through those nearby. My sister darts forward and back, playful, emboldened.

"Careful," my brother says, automatically.

"I'm not far," she replies. "I can still see you."

"That's not the rule," he says.

She spins once, smug. "It's close enough."

Mother watches, says nothing. For a while, the world feels exactly as it always has. Conversations overlap. Someone recounts a ridiculous near-miss from long ago. Someone else exaggerates it shamelessly. Even the elders seem less tense, drifting into easier patterns.

My brother leans closer to me. "When this is over," he says.

"When what's over?" I ask.

He gestures vaguely, encompassing the day, the tension, the unspoken. "When things settle," he says, "I'm going to show you something."

I smile despite myself. "You always say that."

"And I always mean it."

"What is it this time?"

"A place where the current bends," he says. "Not dangerous. Just… different."

The Taking

Mother hears the word different and shifts immediately. "No," she says.

My brother sighs. "I didn't say now."

"I don't care when," Mother replies. "No."

My sister laughs. "You said curiosity wasn't the problem."

"I said distance was," Mother answers. "They're not separate."

My brother softens, as he always does when she speaks like that. "Fine," he says. "I won't go."

Not now, anyway.

The fragments thin and stop. The brightness holds steady, longer than expected. The Many drifts into looser formations, conversations slowing, attention spreading.

It happens in the middle of nothing.

My brother is telling a story—one I've heard before, about the time he misjudged a shift and ended up spinning helplessly until Mother steadied him. He's embellishing shamelessly, using larger gestures than necessary. "And

then," he says, "I realized I wasn't stuck at all. I just needed to stop fighting—"

He doesn't finish. He doesn't pause. He is simply gone.

Not pulled away. Not moved. Not displaced in any way my mind can follow. One moment he is there—warm, familiar, close enough that I can feel the echo of his motion—and the next there is a space. A clean, impossible space. My awareness slams into it like it expects resistance and finds none.

I turn, frantic, searching for where he must have gone, because things don't just end like that.

"—?" My sister tries to say his name and doesn't finish.

Mother moves faster than I've ever seen her move, not toward the space, but toward us— pressing close, anchoring, as if she can physically hold what has already been lost. "No," she says. It is not a command. It is not denial. It is recognition.

The Taking

The world around us tightens violently. Movement fractures. Those nearest pull away instinctively, creating distance without meaning to. The Many ripples with shock, clusters breaking and reforming, fear passing faster than any signal. I stare at the space where my brother was. It does not fill. It does not collapse. It simply is.

My sister makes a sound I have never heard from her before—a thin, broken pressure that sends pain straight through me. "He was right

there," she insists, as if proximity should have mattered.

I move forward without thinking, pushing into the empty place, expecting—hoping—to find some trace of him. There is nothing. No echo. No warmth. Nothing to touch. Mother blocks me gently but firmly, pulling me back.

"Don't," she says. "Don't scatter."

"Where did he go?" my sister demands.

Mother does not answer. She can't. Around us, elders reposition quickly, silently. Someone

murmurs, "Too close," and someone else replies, "No, it was safe," and the words collide uselessly. Old Tareth drifts nearer, his movements heavy with something like sorrow.

"It was fast," he says quietly. "Too fast to feel."

My sister rounds on him. "You didn't see it."

"No," he agrees. "But I felt the absence."

I still can't look away from the space. My mind insists this is wrong. That the world does

not behave this way. That something must follow—some correction, some reversal, some explanation. Nothing comes. Mother presses herself between us and the open stretch now, her presence fierce, contained, breaking only at the edges.

"We stay together," she says. "We don't move. We don't chase what we can't reach."

"He said he wasn't going anywhere," my sister says, her voice sharp with betrayal. "He promised."

Mother closes what passes for her eyes. "I know."

The brightness above us does not change. The world does not react. Fragments do not fall.

Nothing marks what has happened except us. Eventually, the Many settles again—not because the shock fades, but because there is nowhere for it to go. Conversations resume in hushed, altered forms. Laughter does not return.

My sister stays pressed against me, shaking. Mother does not count. She doesn't need to. As the world begins to dim once more, folding inward with its usual indifference, I finally understand something I hadn't before—not fully, not in words, but in the shape of my fear.

The Taking is not something that happens to the world. It is something the world allows. And it does not care who it takes.

We cluster close as the light withdraws, smaller now by one shape we will never stop feeling.

The Taking

Nothing else happens that day. Which feels, somehow, worse.

At night—when the world dims and the Many clusters—my sister presses so close to me that I feel her shaking.

"I didn't say goodbye," she whispers once.

I don't answer, because there isn't one that matters.

Chapter 4
After

The world does not pause for grief. That is the second unbearable thing we learn. Light still arrives when it always has. The rhythm remains exact, indifferent. The Many gathers and disperses, careful now, quieter, shaped

around new absences like a river flowing around missing stones.

My brother's place is never filled. Not by accident. Not by habit. Everyone knows better.

Mother keeps us close. Not visibly tighter—nothing so obvious—but with an awareness that never loosens. She positions herself between us and open stretches. She adjusts when the medium shifts. She anticipates movements before they happen, as if vigilance might become armor if she wears it long enough.

The Taking

My sister changes first. She had always been the one who pushed, who tested distance, who laughed at caution like it was a superstition that didn't deserve her respect. Now she barely drifts beyond arm's reach. When she does, she checks back constantly, as if the world might close behind her the moment she stops looking. At night—when the world dims and the Many clusters—she presses so close to me that I feel her shaking.

"I didn't say goodbye," she whispers once.

I don't answer, because there isn't one that matters.

Mother does not speak my brother's name for a long time. Not because she has forgotten it. Because saying it would make it real in a way she isn't ready to survive.

The elders come, one by one, drifting close enough to acknowledge what has happened without intruding. Old Tareth stays longer than the rest. "It wasn't a failure," he says quietly, when Mother finally looks at him. "It wasn't a mistake."

Mother's attention sharpens. "Then what was it?"

Tareth does not flinch. "It was his time."

My sister turns on him instantly. "Don't say that."

Tareth lowers himself slightly. "I don't mean it cruelly."

"There is no gentle way to say it," my sister replies.

Mother lifts a presence between them, calm but absolute. "Enough."

Tareth nods, accepting the boundary. "We do not control it," he says instead. "We never have. All we control is how we live in between."

After that, no one pretends the rules are suggestions. Movement becomes deliberate. Clusters tighten. The Many feels heavier, denser, as if grief itself has weight. And still—still—the world offers its comforts. Fragments fall from Above. Warmth spreads. The medium carries us when we let it. Life continues, stubbornly, offensively normal.

The Taking

My sister stops laughing. Not entirely. But when she does, it sounds unfamiliar, like she's borrowing the sound from someone else. She drifts less. Watches more. One day, I catch her staring into the space where my brother vanished.

"He said he wasn't stuck," she murmurs.

"I know."

"He said you just had to stop fighting."

I feel something twist inside me. "Maybe he was right."

She looks at me sharply. "About what?"

I don't have an answer. Only a feeling—that the world does not reward resistance, but it does not forgive stillness either.

Mother overhears. "You don't stop moving," she says firmly. "You just move wisely."

"Did he move unwisely?" my sister asks.

Mother does not respond.

That night, as the world dims, I feel it again. The tightening. Subtle. Localized. Like the medium itself drawing in a breath. I freeze. So

does Mother. So does everyone who knows what to feel for. Nothing happens. Not then. Not that night. But the feeling doesn't leave. It lingers over the next days, appearing more often, closer each time. A displacement here. A sudden hush there. A pause in the flow of life that snaps back into place as if embarrassed.

People begin disappearing again. Not near us. Not witnessed. But reported.

"So-and-so hasn't been seen since bright hours." "They were with their kin last night." "They stayed within sight."

No one argues. No one searches. Searching is something you do when you believe there is somewhere to find. Mother grows thinner, not in substance but in presence—stretched, pulled in too many directions at once. I see her counting now, openly, no longer pretending otherwise.

One evening, Old Tareth returns with news he doesn't want to carry. "It's closer," he says simply.

Mother closes herself briefly, gathering strength. "How close?"

"Close enough that pretending otherwise will cost us."

The Many rearranges itself that night. Not dramatically. Just enough to feel it. We cluster deeper into familiar territory. Open stretches remain empty longer. Silence becomes a language. My sister presses against me again.

"If it happens," she says, echoing my brother's words from before, "don't let me go alone."

I turn toward her. "It won't happen."

She gives a small, sad motion that might be a smile. "You don't believe that."

I don't deny it. As the world dims once more, I realize something else, quietly, without panic. We are no longer waiting for the Taking. We are living between each one. And the space between is shrinking.

"Where did you go?" she asks, sharper than usual.

"Not far," I reply. "I just… found something."

Her attention snaps fully to me. "What kind of something?"

I hesitate. "A place that doesn't move."

Chapter 5
The Edges

We begin to notice the boundaries not because we go looking for them, but because we stop going elsewhere. The Many moves less now. Not out of fear exactly—fear would be loud—but out of a shared, unspoken

agreement that distance costs too much. Familiar paths are worn deeper by repetition. Certain stretches remain untouched for entire cycles of light and dimming.

Those stretches feel wrong. Not dangerous. Not threatening. Just… final.

I am the first to linger near one. It happens by accident. I drift farther than intended, following a subtle shift in the medium that feels different from the rest—smoother, quieter, as if the world itself has gone still there. When I stop, I expect to feel movement

continue past me, the familiar give and carry. Instead, I meet resistance. Not force. Not pain. Just an end. I press gently forward. The resistance does not change. It does not yield or flex. It simply exists, absolute and uninterested in negotiation.

I pull back quickly, heart racing. Mother notices immediately. "Where did you go?" she asks, sharper than usual.

"Not far," I reply. "I just… found something."

Her attention snaps fully to me. "What kind of something?"

I hesitate. "A place that doesn't move."

The elders gather soon after. Old Tareth drifts closer than he has in days, his presence heavy.

"We've known about them," he says. "Some of us longer than others."

"Them?" my sister asks.

"The limits," he replies. "The edges."

The Taking

The word spreads quietly through the Many. Not alarmed. Not panicked. Just… acknowledged.

"How many are there?" someone asks.

Tareth doesn't answer immediately. "Enough," he says at last.

Mother presses close to us, protective instinct sharpened into something almost fierce.

"Why didn't you tell us?" my sister demands.

"Because knowing doesn't change them," Tareth replies. "And believing the world was larger helped some of us sleep."

That night, I dream while awake. I drift close to the edge again—not touching this time, just hovering near enough to feel its stillness. The medium behaves strangely there, bending in subtle ways, warping presence and distance. For a moment, I think I see myself reflected back—distorted, doubled, unreal. I retreat before the image can settle.

The Taking

Not long after, we notice the watchers. At first, they are only felt. A pressure from beyond the edge. A vibration that has no source within the world. The light changes suddenly at times, brighter or dimmer without warning, as if something massive has passed between us and whatever gives the world its rhythm. When it happens, everyone stills.

The watchers do not enter. They do not touch. They observe.

"I don't like them," my sister whispers the first time we feel it together.

"They've always been there," Mother replies, though there is no comfort in her voice now.

"They don't help," my sister says.

"No," Mother agrees. "They don't."

Once—only once—I feel something like attention. Not directed exactly at me, but near enough that I cannot pretend it isn't real. The medium trembles faintly, and the edge seems to press inward, as if curious. I pull away, breathless.

The Taking

Later, Old Tareth speaks quietly to Mother. "The one that takes us," he says. "It is also confined."

Mother looks at him sharply. "You don't know that."

"I know it never leaves," he replies. "And I know it appears when the watchers change the world."

Mother is silent for a long time. "So we are not chosen," she says finally. "We are… offered."

Tareth does not correct her.

The Taking happens again soon after. Not to us. Close enough that we feel the absence ripple outward, the sudden thinning of the Many like a bruise spreading under the skin of the world. My sister grips me so tightly I feel her shaking again.

"Don't," she says, not to anyone in particular. "Please don't."

Mother does not move. She does not speak. She simply holds us where we are, as if proximity itself might become a shield.

The Taking

That night, I press close to the edge again—not because I want answers, but because I want to understand the shape of what holds us. The resistance is smooth. Unyielding. Perfectly clear in its refusal. Beyond it, something shifts. A vast shadow passes. And for the first time, I wonder—not with fear, but with a strange, aching clarity—whether the world was ever meant to be endless at all.

"They disturb the world," he says. "And when the world is disturbed, it comes."

My sister turns toward him sharply. "So they cause it?"

"They allow it," he replies. "Which may be worse."

Chapter 6
Everything Aligns

After the edges are named, nothing feels accidental anymore. We still wake. The light still arrives. The fragments still come from Above, indifferent to our grief. But now everything settles into place with a kind of

cruel coherence, as if the world has finally decided to be honest with us.

Mother no longer pretends the edges are distant. She positions us deliberately now, not just away from open stretches but away from the boundaries themselves. When the Many drifts too wide, she signals restraint. When curiosity pulls someone toward the still places, elders redirect without explanation. No one argues. Understanding has replaced debate.

My sister grows quieter still. Not withdrawn—never that—but focused, like

someone listening for a sound no one else hears.

"They're closer," she says one day.

"Who?" I ask, though I know.

"The watchers."

She's right. The vibrations come more often now. Subtle at first—changes in pressure, brief flickers of light—but growing bolder, more intrusive. The world brightens too suddenly or dims too fast, as if controlled by a will that does not belong to it. Each time it happens, the

Taking follows soon after. Never immediately. Always close enough to be undeniable.

Old Tareth confirms it in a voice that carries no triumph in being right. "They disturb the world," he says. "And when the world is disturbed, it comes."

My sister turns toward him sharply. "So they cause it?"

"They allow it," he replies. "Which may be worse."

Mother listens in silence, her presence taut.

The Taking

"Then why don't they stop it?" I ask.

Tareth's gaze drifts toward the edge. "Because stopping it would require seeing us as something other than we are."

The answer settles heavily. I begin to notice patterns. Not just in when the Taking happens, but in who is taken. It is not random—not entirely. Those who wander more. Those who linger near the boundaries. Those who hesitate when the world shifts instead of moving with it. And yet, sometimes, it takes those who do

none of those things. Because patterns do not guarantee mercy.

One evening, as the world dims, my sister presses close. "Do you remember what he said?" she asks.

"I remember everything," I reply.

"He said the world wasn't as small as we pretend."

I don't answer immediately.

"She was right too," my sister continues softly. "About distance."

The Taking

"Yes," I say.

She shifts, restless. "I think both can be true."

That night, I drift alone for the first time since my brother was taken. Not far. Not recklessly. Just enough to feel the shape of my own presence again. I stop near the edge. I don't touch it. I don't need to. The resistance is there regardless, smooth and final and perfectly clear. But something else is clearer now too—the way the medium bends near it,

how movement distorts, how the world feels thinner, almost transparent.

Beyond the edge, a shadow passes. This time, I don't recoil. I stay still. And for a brief, impossible moment, I feel seen. Not known. Not understood. Just noticed. The attention passes quickly, replaced by the familiar indifference that has shaped our lives from the beginning. I return to my family shaken, but certain.

The world is not failing us. It is functioning exactly as it was built to. The predator does not

hate us. The watchers do not judge us. No one is cruel here. And that is the most terrible truth of all.

Later, when the next Taking happens—and it does, closer now, close enough that we feel the absence tear through the Many like a wound—Mother finally speaks the words she has been avoiding.

"There is no safe place," she says quietly. "Only time."

My sister presses her presence against mine. "How much?"

Mother closes herself briefly, then opens again. "Less than we hoped."

We cluster that night tighter than ever before, a small knot of living warmth in a world that no longer pretends to be infinite. As the light withdraws and the world folds inward, I understand something else—not all at once, not with clarity, but with a steady, settling certainty. The edges are not there to protect us. They are there to contain us. And whatever lives with us here—lives here because of them.

Now that I see it clearly, I understand why it was never described properly. It is not monstrous. It is not malicious. It is ancient in the way tools are ancient—built for one purpose and incapable of questioning it. Its movements are swift, decisive, efficient.

Chapter 7

The Reality of the World

The end does not arrive suddenly. It arrives all at once.

The light changes without warning—not the usual dimming, not the familiar rhythm. It brightens sharply, too bright, as if the world

has been pulled closer to something vast and exposed. The Many stills. The edges tremble. And for the first time, the watchers do not remain distant.

A shape looms beyond the boundary— enormous, layered, impossible to comprehend all at once. I feel its presence not as threat, but as scale. Perspective. A reminder of how small everything has always been. Mother presses close instinctively. My sister does the same.

"Something's wrong," my sister whispers.

The Taking

"No," Mother says, and her voice is steady in a way that finally frightens me. "Something is clear."

The world shifts. Not violently. Precisely. The medium surges, displaced by a force that does not belong to us but moves among us anyway. It arrives with speed so sudden there is no time to react, no moment to flee. The predator is there. Not emerging. Not approaching. Simply present.

Now that I see it clearly, I understand why it was never described properly. It is not

monstrous. It is not malicious. It is ancient in the way tools are ancient—built for one purpose and incapable of questioning it. Its movements are swift, decisive, efficient.

It feeds.

The watchers beyond the edge lean closer. I feel their attention sharpen, curious but detached, as if observing a process rather than a tragedy. And suddenly—everything aligns. The fragments from Above. The rhythm of the light. The smooth, unmoving edges. The

predator that appears when the world is disturbed.

This is not a world. We are contained—inside.

The edges are not stone or distance or the end of possibility. They are clear. Perfectly clear. I see my reflection in them at last—not metaphorical, not imagined, but real and unmistakable. A small body, bright and fragile, shaped for motion in this medium.

The predator pivots, impossibly fast, its armored body and scaled legs moving with practiced ease.

The watchers shift again, and the world trembles with their movement. A face presses closer to the boundary—vast, curious, utterly removed.

Understanding crashes through me like cold clarity. We were never meant to escape. We were never meant to fight. We were never meant to understand. We were meant to

exist—briefly, beautifully—inside someone else's world.

Mother is taken first. There is no warning. No time to call out. One moment she is there—anchoring us, holding the shape of our family together—and the next she is gone, collected with the same indifferent speed that has governed every loss before her. My sister screams. I feel it tear through the medium, raw and helpless.

She turns toward me, eyes wide, unanchored. "Don't let me—" She does not finish.

The predator moves again. I am alone.

The Many is nearly gone now—only a handful remain, scattered, silent, no longer pretending at normalcy. The watchers withdraw slightly, interest waning. The light steadies. The world resumes.

I drift near the edge, pressed close to the clear boundary, feeling its smooth refusal beneath me. Beyond it, the Watcher turns

away, satisfied. The predator settles back into stillness, hunger temporarily sated. For a long moment, nothing happens. I am not taken. I am left.

And in that quiet, I understand the final truth. The predator was never the villain. The Watcher was never a deity. The boundary was never the enemy. They are all just parts of a system that does not know our names.

We loved anyway. We stayed close. We remembered one another. For a time, that was enough.

The light dims again, returning to its familiar rhythm. The world folds inward, smaller now, emptier. I drift alone in the medium, the last bright flicker of a life that was never meant to be noticed.

And yet—I was here.

www.ingramcontent.com/pod-product-compliance
Lightning Source LLC
Chambersburg PA
CBHW051144020726
47501CB00005B/1676